Magrit

LEE BATTERSBY

MAGRIT

WITH ILLUSTRATIONS BY

AMY DAOUD

WALKER BOOKS
AND SUBSIDIARIES
LONDON • BOSTON • SYDNEY • AUCKLAND

First published in 2016
by Walker Books Australia Pty Ltd
Locked Bag 22, Newtown
NSW 2042 Australia
www.walkerbooks.com.au

National Library of Australia Cataloguing-in-Publication entry:
Battersby, Lee, 1970– author.
Magrit / Lee Battersby; Amy Daoud.
ISBN: 978 1 925081 34 3 (hardback)
For children.
Subjects: Paranormal fiction, Australian.
Fantasy fiction, Australian.
Other Creators/Contributors: Daoud, Amy, illustrator.
A823.4

Typeset in Adobe Caslon Pro
Printed and bound in China

TO ERIN AND CONNOR,
IN THE HOPES THAT
THEIR JOURNEYS OF
DISCOVERY WILL UNCOVER
BOUNDLESS WONDERS,
AND THAT ALL WINDOWS
WILL LEAD TO NEW
WORLDS.

ONE RAINY SPRING NIGHT WHEN she was nearly ten years old, a girl named Magrit climbed onto the roof of the chapel at the centre of the octagonal cemetery that was her home. She nestled herself against a tall, skeletal figure that gazed out across the grounds like an ancient guardian. Together, they bathed in the light that shimmered through the curtains of the surrounding buildings.

The skeleton's name was Master Puppet. Magrit had pieced him together from elements she had found in every corner of the graveyard: a bone here, a stick there, a tin can in one corner and rotten twine from a garbage bag in another. Now he sat at the apex of the roof, with his long arms wrapped around the stone cross, and kept vigil.

"Look at that sky," Magrit said to Master Puppet. "It looks sick and old, and fallen to the ground to die."

"Yes, it does look lovely, doesn't it?" said Master Puppet. When he talked, he did so in Magrit's voice, only deeper and grown-up. Magrit often asked him for advice. Unlike the gargoyles and rats, he usually answered.

"Will you be all right in the rain?" she asked.

Master Puppet harrumphed. "I am unconcerned about the likelihood of impending damage." Master Puppet liked to use words Magrit heard filtering out

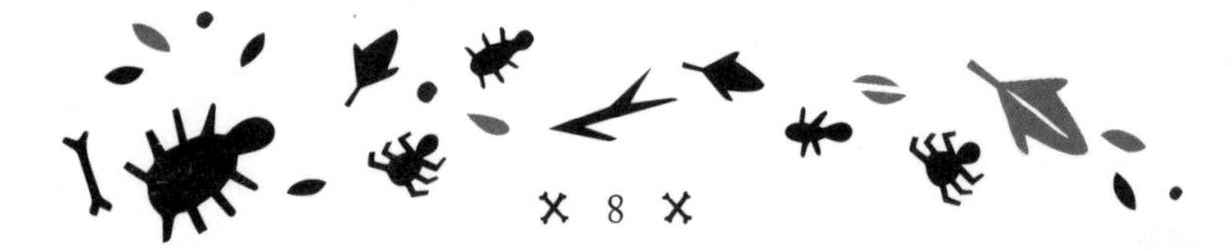

through the windows around them, even if he did sometimes forget how they were pronounced, or if neither of them knew *quite* what they meant.

"THE RAIN WATERS THE DEAD THINGS BELOW US AND KEEPS THEM IN THEIR PLACE."

Magrit looked down at the ground. The gravel paths were thick with weeds and scuttling things that rattled the tiny stones together as if they were bones in the wind. Headstones emerged from the grass: eyeless skulls that peered over the withered stalks. "Why do we need to keep the dead things in place?"

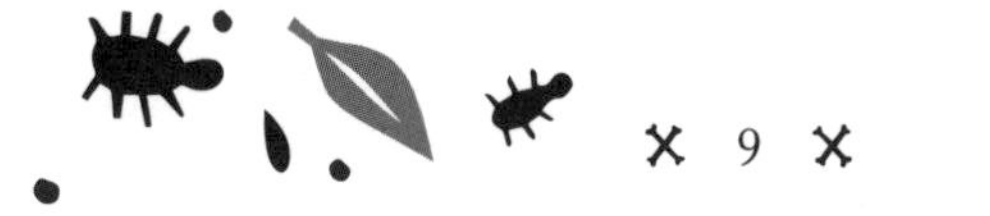

Master Puppet sighed. "We've discussed this before," he said. "Everything must have its place. The dead stay below. The buildings surround us. The sky remains above. And we stay in between, unseen and undiscovered and safe, as it should be."

Magrit knew he was right. The chapel they were perched on was a small structure, surrounded by knee-high yellow grass and dwarfed by the cold grey apartment buildings that circled it like bullies. The paths that ran from the chapel to the edges of the cemetery led to exits that had long ago been blocked off by the rise of the apartments. There was no way to enter, or leave. The cemetery crouched between the high walls, and the darkness of their shadows wrapped Magrit in secrets and safety. It was home, and Magrit loved it with the fierce love that comes with complete possession.

"What about the stars?" Magrit asked for no particular reason, except that on a night like tonight, with the rain forming a gentle curtain between her and the clouds, it was easy to imagine that the stars had drawn blankets up over themselves and gone to sleep.

"The stars are of no consequence," said Master Puppet.

"What about that one?" she asked, pointing upwards.

Up above, a white shape flapped laboriously over the rooftops, shaking and shivering in the thin, wet air. Something small dropped from its front end and disappeared onto the roof of the nearest building. The white shape circled it for a minute or two, then raced off over the blackening sky.

"That was not a star," Master Puppet said.

"What was it?"

"A stork," he replied. "Filthy beast of a thing."

"Why is it filthy?"

Master Puppet contemplated her with his big black eye sockets. "Because," he said, his bony jaw hanging loose and yellow under his skull, "storks bring new life to the world, and that sort of thing has *no* place in a cemetery such as ours."

"Oh."

A small grey bundle rolled down the slick incline of the roof. It trundled into the gutter, rode the gushing water to the top of the downpipe, then disappeared inside. A moment later it popped out the bottom. A fountain had fallen over so that its bowl lay beneath the pipe opening and was now no more than a concrete dish, sitting on the ragged lawn. The bundle splashed down into it and bobbed to the rim, before the flow of water dropped it, squalling, into the long grass beneath.

"And what's that?"

Master Puppet was silent for a long time, so that Magrit began to wonder if he had not heard her. She was about to repeat her question when he spoke into her mind, his voice whispery and a bit scared.

"It's a horrible thing," he said over the bundle's screeches.

"An awful, ugly, TERRIBLE thing."

His bones rattled in the breeze. "Get rid of it. Throw it away. Kill it."

"But what *is* it?"

Master Puppet would not answer. Eventually, Magrit grew tired of asking. She slipped down the slimy, moss-heavy roof, dropped to the ground and stomped her way over to the squawking, wriggling bundle.

"It's breathing!" she called.

Master Puppet said nothing. Magrit pursed her lips and crept closer. When she was less than three steps away, she kneeled down, not caring that the hem of her dress, which she had only found in a brand-new, undiscovered vault a few days ago, would get muddied in the wet grass. Cautiously, she reached out a hand and gave the cloth package a poke.

"It's squishy!"

The parcel screamed. Magrit fell backwards in fright. She landed in a puddle and jumped up, patting her wet bum cheeks in disgust.

Master Puppet's leathery, whispering voice called out to her. "You see?" he said. "I told you …"

Magrit grunted and bent over the cotton-wrapped mystery. She turned her body so Master Puppet could not see her fingers tremble, took hold of the edge of the cloth – so very like a shroud, it was – and peeled it back.

Despite the darkness of night, Margit could see something pink and wriggly and naked inside. Its chubby arms and legs waved back and forth like an overturned beetle. She peered at its scrunched-up eyes and the nose that dribbled a watery line of snot, and its toothless mouth opening and closing and making bubbles of spit on its bobbly chin. As she looked at its shiny pink and white body, it fell still and opened its eyes at her. Magrit gulped. The creature started to wee. Magrit shuffled out of the way.

"It's a baby!" she called back to Master Puppet. "A proper living boy baby."

"I know what it is, stupid girl." Master Puppet sounded angry and not at all pleased that she was able to identify the new arrival. "I told you what it was."

"No, you didn't. You said it was horrible and terrible." The baby had stopped weeing. Magrit studied his tiny little face. "He doesn't look horrible to me."

"Oh, no?" Her friend sounded huffy. Master Puppet didn't like it when Magrit disagreed with him. She didn't do it very often. "You just wait until it starts to poo!"

Magrit ignored him. The baby was making rhythmic squealing noises now, drawing in breath in short, gasping bursts then opening up his mouth so wide she could see his tiny tongue pressed hard against the roof of his mouth. For the first time, she began to worry about the buildings around her, and what might happen if the baby's noise should cause the people inside to look out at them.

"What do I do with it?" she asked.

"I'm not going to kill it. That would be ..." Actually, Magrit didn't know what it would be. She was going to say "cruel", but she didn't really think death *was* cruel. The cemetery was full of dead things. Death was normal. It was *life* she did not understand. She had hardly any experience of it.

Magrit had been born in one of the apartments overlooking the cemetery, although she could recall nothing beyond the cold concrete floor and the sharp-edged plastic furniture, and the constant smell of cigarette smoke and chip fat. But Magrit did not care to think about it too much. She had spent what life she could remember surrounded by dead people, and their company was just as she wished it to be. They didn't seem unhappy. Dead people didn't get cold, or tired, or skin their knees and bleed. They didn't get thirsty or itchy or get rashes on their bottoms or have sore gums or stub their toes. They didn't stamp their feet and hit the dried grass with their fists and toss their heads when they didn't get their own way. They didn't act like Magrit at all. They simply lay very still and very quiet and let rats use their skulls as homes and every now and again gnaw their bones. Dead people never complained and they never cried. Killing the baby would not be cruel. It would be … what?

"It would be … wrong," she finished. Before Master Puppet could ask what was so wrong about it she picked up the baby and held him to her chest.

"You touched it!" Master Puppet cried in outrage. "You went and touched it! Now you'll have its smell on you! You'll … you'll … smell like a *person*!"

Magrit stared into the baby's eyes. The baby peered back. "I don't care," she whispered. She had never defied Master Puppet before. She risked a glance at him. "I think he's hungry."

Master Puppet refused to answer. Magrit leaned over the baby, protecting him from the rain.

"And he needs a name."

"Dead things," Master Puppet's voice dripped with anger and scorn, "do not *require* names."

"He's not dead."

"He will be. Then what good will a name do him?"

"*You* have one."

After that, Master Puppet didn't talk to her for *hours*.

+X+

MAGRIT WAS RIGHT, OF COURSE. The baby *was* hungry. Magrit stepped away from the shelter of the chapel and carried him around. He shrieked with a voice so shrill, it had her dreading the idea of lights going on in windows all around the cemetery. Magrit rocked him as gently as she could, her eyes flitting from window to window in panic. All her life she had feared the cold, blank faces of glass. It was a lesson she held deep within her bones: do not disturb those who live behind the curtains. Do not draw their attention. To be discovered was to be ruined, to have her world crash down upon her and all her special places and secrets and thoughts stripped from her. But the baby would not stop crying, and now, as she had feared, the unseen strangers behind the windows were shouting at each other.

"Shut that damn baby up! People are trying to sleep!"

"Shut your own baby up!"

"You shut up!"

"*You* shut up!"

"Shut that ruddy baby up!"

Magrit gawked at the surrounding walls. The world she lived in was a fragile one. Nobody visited her. Nobody from the surrounding buildings saw her.

The lonely graves only ever felt a human touch when someone threw a garbage bag out of their window, to split and spray rubbish across the layers and layers of trash that had come before.

A single white face at the glass, one hidden resident discovering just what occupied the land between the tall brick buildings; one sight of the willowy almost-ten-year-old girl clutching the screaming infant to her chest, and Magrit's happy life would come to an end. All it needed was for someone to stop shouting and look out of the window. She had to feed the baby *something*, to quieten him. But she didn't know what babies ate. Master Puppet was her only teacher, and when it came to subjects outside the immediate world of gravel paths and fallen headstones, he tended to be vague and evasive.

The only education she received that did not come from Master Puppet was from watching television through the partly open curtains of the surrounding tenements and, even then, she often had to make sense of the images alone if the volume was low.

And none of it helped her to work out what to do with the baby. All she could go on were dim memories of her early life and the food she gathered as she rummaged desperately through the piles of refuse between the gravestones. Magrit had always been able to feed herself. There was plenty of food on the ground, even if some of it was stale or a bit rotten around the edges. Occasionally, rats fought hard for their share of scraps, so she regularly retreated to the chapel with half the food she wanted and her arms covered in scratches and bites. With time, she had learned to avoid the nastier ones and grew used to the feel of their feet on her face as she slept.

As she had grown older and more capable, she learned to bend her world to her needs. When she was dirty she found that rain was very much like a shower, and the sun was a lot better than a stiff rub with a towel. The crypts gave her clothes to wear, even if she had to give them a good shaking first, just to make sure all the bones were out of them. If she was cold, she wrapped herself up in a nest she made from shrouds. If she was thirsty, she drank from rainwater that splashed into the fountains and fonts scattered throughout the grounds.

She had almost a whole life of hard-won knowledge at her disposal. But none of it was proving useful. The baby didn't seem to want to eat. Holding him out of the rain as best she could, she crawled from rubbish bag to rubbish bag, rummaging through them in the dark. She found bread crusts to tempt him with, but he showed no interest. He cried when she tried to put an apple core in his mouth. He refused to consider the half a fish finger with cold egg yolk on it. Magrit ate that one herself. She wasn't going to miss out on a treat like *that* if she didn't have to.

But still the baby cried. More and more windows were lighting up. Magrit cradled the baby in the crook of her stomach. She had to feed him *something*. Anything would do, as long as she could persuade him to eat it. She headed back towards the cracked concrete path that ran in a rough circle between the fields of graves. Her foot came down on something soft and wriggling. She pressed down, and it squished up between her toes as her weight crushed it flat against the stone. A goopy grey mass was bubbling up between her toes. The rain had brought out a writhing blanket of worms, and she had stepped onto a whole bed of them, squelching them to paste.

She looked at the mushed-up worms. She looked at the baby. She looked at the worms again. She began to smile.

Magrit shuffled across to a nearby headstone and sat cross-legged upon it. She arranged the baby in her lap and carefully scooped the tiniest bit of worm paste onto the end of her finger. Then she pressed it against the baby's mouth, and held her breath as he sucked at it. She took her finger out slowly. The baby kept sucking for a few seconds before he realised the finger wasn't there. He screwed up his little face. Magrit scraped up some more worm paste. The baby gulped it down, and again and again, until all of the squelched-up worms were gone and he finally, quietly, fell asleep.

Magrit felt a warm stirring of pride deep within her chest. She could feed a baby. She could do it all by herself, with no help or advice from Master Puppet or anybody else. She glanced towards her friend at the top of the church building. She could see the rain threading through the gaps in his skeleton and tiny rivulets flowing down from his eye sockets like tears. She wanted to call out to him, to tell him that he was her best and only friend, and nothing would ever change that, not even a baby.

He was still ignoring her, so she said nothing.

Magrit blew Master Puppet a tiny raspberry. He was just stroppy because he had thought she couldn't feed the baby, and she had. There was something else Master Puppet had said, something else he thought she couldn't do. Magrit looked down at the sleeping baby's face. What was it?

A name. That was it. She couldn't keep thinking of the baby as "him" or "the baby". Magrit frowned. She didn't know any names. She knew how Master Puppet got his and hers was a half-remembered scrap of a name she would no longer recognise if it was given to her.

Magrit decided to do what she always did when she was in search of an answer. The night was well advanced, but she could hear the murmur of televisions from the nearby windows. She could climb the slippery roofs of the crypts, one by one, and peer through the minute gaps in the curtains. Perhaps she might find a show about babies. Perhaps the sound would be turned up loud enough for her to hear a name or two. But the baby was sleeping and she didn't want to risk waking him up.

Magrit wriggled her bum about to get comfortable. There didn't seem anything nearby that lent itself to a baby name. She didn't want to call him "grass" or "rubbish" or "plastic bag". That would be confusing when she wanted to talk about *real* grass or rubbish or plastic bags. Master Puppet might have some great ideas – he certainly knew a lot of words she didn't, and liked to use them when he wanted to appear particularly clever – but she'd get no help out of him while he was in this mood. She wrinkled her nose and whisked away a mosquito from the baby's face. The mosquito zipped off and, in that instant, she knew what she would do.

"That's it!"

Somewhere at the edge of her mind she heard a quiet "Harrumph" in Master Puppet's voice. Magrit ignored him. She had her solution. At least, she had the beginning of one. If the baby had to have a name, *he* should be the one to choose it.

How, though? She didn't think he could speak. Not in words. She'd seen him wave his arms about but it didn't look like he could point very well. So, if the baby had no way of telling her what he had chosen, perhaps she could see whether something might choose him instead. She knew he would cry if he was unhappy, so if he didn't cry, then surely that must mean he was happy. If the world gave him a name and he didn't howl about it, she would know it was the right one. Magrit grinned. That was clever, grown-up thinking, the kind that Master Puppet kept all to himself.

She laid the cotton wrap on the concrete next to her, where the lee of two crossed headstones provided a shallow shelter from the rain. She lifted the baby from her lap, placed him in the middle, and tucked the wrap around him so that only his sleeping face was visible. Then she took up position on her tummy, and waited.

Whatever touched his face first, she decided. That's what his name would be. No. She changed her mind. The first *two* things. That way she'd have two different things to call him, and it would stop her confusing the baby with the original objects.

The first two things to touch the baby's face would give him his new name.

And that's how he came to be called Bugrat.

THE SHAPE OF MAGRIT'S LIFE changed. Bugrat was a hungry baby, and where once she filled her day with games of Pitch Pebble and Fountain Splash, Tickle Rat and Headstone Hop, now she was constantly on the hunt for worms to squish. At first it was fun, like a game of Rubbish Hunt but with only one type of rubbish to hunt. But Bugrat wanted feeding four or five or six times every day, and as many times again during the night. Soon the game stopped being a game: it took her away from her own things, until all she ever did was feed the baby, clean him up and feed him again.

And, oh my goodness, the poo! Master Puppet had been right about the poo. It seemed that the dawn brought the poo with it, because as soon as the light of the morning crested the surrounding buildings, Bugrat yawned, stretched until his face turned red with effort, and delivered a loud, squelching, squirty poo that came out and out and out as if it was never going to end.

At first, Magrit hadn't known what to do with it. She tried splashing Bugrat with water from a puddle, cooing and humming TV tunes in the hope that he would ignore the feel of icy water on his legs and bottom and concentrate on her not-at-all happy smile above him. He had not been fooled, and her efforts only made him cry harder. Then she had tried rubbing his bum with a torn pillowcase, but all that did was spread the poo over the baby and the pillowcase as well. In the end, she chose a font near the centre of the cemetery and used it as a bath, ignoring his squeals of displeasure until the whole unpleasant task was completed.

When she was done she had wrapped him up, hugged him against her bony chest until he fell asleep, and then spent an unpleasant hour scooping the mucky water onto the grass below. The font would refill the next time there was rain. But she would never again use it for drinking water. She had wrinkled her mouth in disgust and stood back, counting the fonts around her. As long as the baby only pooed twice a day, she had calculated, and it rained about once a week, things might be okay.

"I told you," said a leathery voice, from up where Master Puppet sat. "I warned you."

This time, Magrit had not spoken to *him*.

Today, after her bottom-washing routine, Magrit carried the sleeping baby into the nearest vault, away from Master Puppet's contemplation and his humourless chuckle. She sank down into a dry corner, placed Bugrat in her lap and rested her head against the stone sarcophagus inside. Magrit did not often cry. But she was tired. Very, very tired.

She had not been so tired in a long time. Not since she had wandered through the grass one day, when the cemetery was much, much younger. Magrit tried never to think of that day, or the corner behind the chapel. There was something in that corner, something that made her mind buck and shy away. At the edge of her memory, she recalled feeling hot, like she was wearing a blanket inside her body, and her eyes being so heavy she could not keep them open. She remembered lying down on the cool ground, remembered closing her eyes and sleeping so long it felt like tens of years passed before she heard Master Puppet's voice calling out within her mind. She woke to find the graveyard sunk in shadow. She had never gone back to that place. And she had never been so tired again, until now, holding Bugrat in her heavy arms.

All she needed was a nap, she told herself. Just to close her eyes and nap. Trying to nap when the baby was sleeping was what she did now, as often as she could. An hour here, an hour there. She was beginning to lose the hang of sleeping properly.

She wished she knew if this was how mothers felt, but every time she tried to remember her own mother, all she could recall was the sound of a worn-out voice always shouting at someone or other. She didn't like the memory. It grated against her mind, like the caw of the crows she sometimes had to scare away to get to the freshest rubbish. She shifted against the stone and tightened her grip on Bugrat. She didn't want to be a mummy with a crow voice. She would nap when she could, and always, *always* be happy.

Being always happy was sometimes hard, especially when she had to do it for months on end, and even more especially when, in late autumn, Bugrat's teeth started to come through, and all she could do was let him nip at her fingers to soothe his pain and not cry out when he drew blood. Or when he started to crawl and scurried away to some corner when she wasn't looking and cut himself on a sharp-cornered bag of refuse.

On those days she would glance down at her own scarred and ragged knees and sigh. She had survived similar escapades and grown to be almost ten, hadn't she? It was all just part of growing up, she knew, all just part of claiming her world as his own.

The tiredness never quite went away. It became a fact of life, as much as her bones and her skin and the scratch on her finger that never quite healed. And despite her constant tiredness and the sleepless nights and the endless fear of discovery and the worry that she was doing everything wrong, there *were* happy times.

One night, nine months after his arrival, Magrit carried Bugrat into their favourite sleeping crypt, and snuggled him into a thick nest of rags she had assembled to ward off the cold of the winter just past. As he lay silent, with his big eyes watching her solemnly, she wrapped rags tighter and tighter around him, crooning a half-remembered rhyme from her long-ago life.

"Snug as a Bugrat with a grub ..."

Suddenly, he wriggled his arms free and lunged towards her. Before she could react, he pressed his chubby hands into her cheeks and bumped his face against hers. His lips, wet and sloppy with the drool that always coated his chin, pressed against hers for a fleeting second. Then he lay down, and regarded her. Magrit stared at him for long seconds, then bit her lower lip and leaned down to kiss him.

"I love you," she said.

She gazed into his eyes hopefully. She didn't need him to say the words or even attempt to. A single noise would have been enough to fill her heart. But Bugrat stayed silent.

"Just once? Say it once?" she said. In the end, all she could do was hold him as his eyes fluttered, and closed, and his soft breaths deepened and flattened into snoring.

When she was sure he was asleep, she crept out of the crypt and stood beneath the dim outline of Master Puppet on his roof.

"He kissed me."

Master Puppet said nothing.

"He loves me."

"How nice for you." His voice was neutral, showing no emotion, saying nothing beyond the flat, grey reality of his words. Magrit sighed, then hung her head, and gave up her tiny pretence of rebellion.

"Why won't he speak to me?"

"PERHAPS HE HAS nothing TO SAY TO YOU."

Magrit bit down on the angry, hurtful words she wanted to scream.

Eventually, in the calmest, most even voice she had ever used, she said, "You are supposed to be my friend. And you've never kissed me. Never even once. You've never given me a nuzzly hug, or wrapped your fingers around one of mine while you fell asleep. We've never played tickling games in the dark. You've never made me giggle and giggle and giggle. You've never done anything."

"Haven't I?"

Magrit's fists were clenched so tight they hurt. She pinned them to the sides of her legs, so that they wouldn't do anything she might regret. "Bugrat got so excited the first time I held a rat and let him stroke its fur, he weed himself. And the first time he held a spare crust of bread in his hand and let a raven peck it out, he squeezed my arm so hard, I could see his finger marks on my skin for *ages*."

"Happy days."

"All you do." Her legs were quivering, and Magrit locked her knees together. "That's all you do. You sit there, above me. Making nasty comments. Criticising me. Sniping and putting me down and talking to me like I'm a silly girl who has to be told I'm stupid all the time. You don't even … You've never …"

She wanted to say, "You don't love me. You've never loved me." But she couldn't bring herself to say it. Something inside her knew that if she did, she would cross some invisible line that she could never un-cross. For all his faults, she knew the charge of lovelessness wasn't true.

Master Puppet did love her.

His love was real, but it was a cold, hard skeletal love.

Now, while the sun shone weakly through the smog layer and bathed the graveyard in its thin grey radiance, he said nothing. When the cold of the night became too much like the cold of their anger at each other, she spun on her heel and stalked away, back to the crypt and her own nest of rags.

It was only when she was safely burrowed beneath them, and had turned her face into the stone corner, that Master Puppet's dry voice slithered down between the gaps in the stone towards her. "What do you think you're doing?" he asked. "What do you think is going to happen?"

She did not answer him. Right now all she wanted to do was sleep. Master Puppet always had to be right, to get the last word in. His body was soaked in all the wisdom and knowledge the graveyard had absorbed over the centuries. Parts of him were so old Magrit could not count that high. He couldn't stop acting like a grown-up even if he wanted to.

"What's going to happen when it's not a baby any more? What's going to happen when it grows up? What if it wants to leave? What will you do if it stops liking you? What will you do if it goes away?"

"He's not an it. He's a *he*."

"Everything is an it, at one level or another. And what will you do when it realises

YOU ARE JUST an it AS WELL?"

Even when she was ignoring him, Master Puppet's questions knocked at her ears like unwelcome visitors, refusing to go away until she answered the door and let them in.

+X+

EVER SINCE SHE FIRST ARRIVED in the cemetery, Magrit had named things that had no names, and discovered things that had lain undisturbed for centuries, to understand her world and growing to fit it like someone born to live there. There was a lot of fun to be had in Magrit's cemetery, especially when the rain stopped and she could invent games with the puddles that pooled across the uneven concrete, jumping over and around, and most fun of all, into them. Then she could swish through the long grass and swipe up droplets from their tips, laughing as the spray tickled the inside of her wrists. She would hop from fallen headstone to headstone, or climb the walls of the crypts like a spider and pitch pebbles into the middle of the cemetery before counting how long it took her to race through the graves and find them. And the cemetery wrapped its cold, grey arms around her, and gave her what protection it could.

All of these things were fun when Magrit was alone, but now that she had Bugrat to share them, they became more exciting than she had ever dreamed possible. Because he was too small to climb the crypt walls, she took to throwing pebbles at ground level and discovered a new game when she flung one into a vault and they crawled through the deep shadows within, racing to see who could find it first and win a big hug and kiss. Bugrat had not yet learned to walk, so rather than jump between headstones, she picked him up and swooshed him from stone to stone as if he was flying like the birds they sometimes saw between the roofs. And where she once attacked the rubbish bags in fierce abandon, flicking unwanted trash to either side in her search for food, now she carefully sorted through them, wary of hitting the crawling baby beside her.

And because she was careful, and took time to examine the treasures she uncovered, instead of cramming down the first edible thing she chanced upon, she found tomato plants that had sprung from long-discarded seeds and now fruited against the walls, as well as potatoes and onions that budded and bloomed underneath the rotting compost of her discards. She ate fresh vegetables for the first time, and tears rolled down her cheeks for no reason she could understand except that everything tasted so firm and clean and fresh.

If she was teaching Bugrat to walk and explore and

discover the world around him, then he was teaching her patience and care in return.

She exposed watermelons and pumpkins and capsicum, small and stunted and crawling with tiny flies, but to a girl who had only ever known the taste of rot and fungus and mould, they were a treasure without compare. Even Master Puppet smiled inside her head and said, "Well done, you clever girl," when she showed him.

"It was Bugrat," she replied. "He showed me what I was missing."

"DID HE JUST?"

"Yes." She turned to Bugrat. "Didn't you?"

But Bugrat said nothing, simply played with his fingers.

Magrit's smile faltered. "He never says anything."

"There will come a time," Master Puppet replied, his voice flat and unemotional.

"A time for what?"

"A time to speak."

"When? When is he going to say something?"

Master Puppet said no more, so Magrit put it from her mind, and returned her attentions to the boy.

They passed their days in relative happiness, and gradually Master Puppet began to accept Bugrat into their lives as if he had always been there. He questioned Magrit less at night, and occasionally called the baby "Bugrat" instead of just "it". When she caught him silently guarding Bugrat as he played alone in the grass in front of the chapel without making sarcastic comments to her about her parenting, she knew that what had once been a family of two people, and had then been a family of two *different* people, was now a family of three.

+X+

ONE DAY, WHEN BUGRAT HAD lived with them for almost a year, and Magrit was almost ten, he crawled to her across the floor of the crypt, took a handful of her skirt, and pulled himself to his feet. He glanced up at Magrit with a look of joyful concentration, rocked his foot off the ground and took a single, solitary step before falling to his knees. Magrit scooped him up and ran outside.

"Master Puppet! Master Puppet!"

Master Puppet stared down at her from his perch. "What is it, child?"

"Watch." She placed Bugrat on the ground and stepped half-a-dozen paces back. "See what he just did."

Bugrat crawled across to her. He pulled himself up and took another small step.

"Did you see?" Magrit asked. "Did you see him do it?"

"I did," Master Puppet said slowly. "You are going to have to keep a much closer eye on your young ward from now on."

"What do you mean?" Magrit asked.

"The child lacks reason, and requires a physical guardian as well as a moral one. I can only provide one of those services."

Magrit wrinkled her nose. Master Puppet was using grown-up words again, trying to confuse her, to make her feel small and stupid so she would stop asking questions. But she had grown up, just a bit, looking after Bugrat. She could ask grown-up questions too.

"To where do you reference?"

Master Puppet sighed. "Refer," he said.

"AND I REFER TO THE PLACE OF OVERGROWN GRASS AND HIDDEN SECRETS. YOU KNOW TO WHERE I REFER."

Magrit felt a cold caterpillar crawl up the back of her neck. She began to turn her head towards the corner of the cemetery behind the chapel.

"He wouldn't," she whispered. "He *wouldn't*." But Master Puppet simply stared at Bugrat so that

Magrit imagined she could see a thoughtful frown on his skull. She whirled around and picked Bugrat up. "He's just jealous," she whispered to him in an angry hiss as she stalked away. Away from the cold corner that clamoured after her attention. Away from the new noise that called at the edge of her hearing, like Magrit's own voice but weak and wavering. Magrit knew she should have stopped and investigated, but she was too angry at Master Puppet to really pay attention. She had to get away from him. "*He* can't stand up, *or* crawl, much less walk. He never even climbed up to the top of the chapel. I did that; yes, I did." She glanced up at the gaunt, empty figure, draped over the large stone cross at the front of the roof. "I clambered up that crumbly stone wall and dragged him from crack to crevice. I hung his arms over that cross. I held his head until he could look over the grounds by himself. He can't do *anything*. And I can walk wherever *I* want to."

Something whispered in the back of her mind,

a ghost of sound. Magrit ignored it, ignored the tiny corner behind the chapel that said, *No, no, you can't. You can go anywhere but here.*

She wandered deep into the cemetery, where she trampled down a patch of grass and spent the afternoon playing games with Bugrat. In the end, tired out by his exertions, he curled up on the soft grass and fell asleep. Magrit lay down beside him with her eyes closed and felt the breeze tickle her face. She loved to feel it tiptoeing around her, day or night, without ever once pausing to say hello. The wind had its own business to attend to, and rarely stopped to chat. She cupped her hands behind her head and chewed on a stalk of long grass and daydreamed.

Sometimes, Magrit wondered what existed beyond the boundaries of her brick-clad universe. There had to be *something*; she knew that without being sure how she knew. She had seen birds flying across the broad circle of sky between buildings, and it stood to reason that they had to come from somewhere and were going

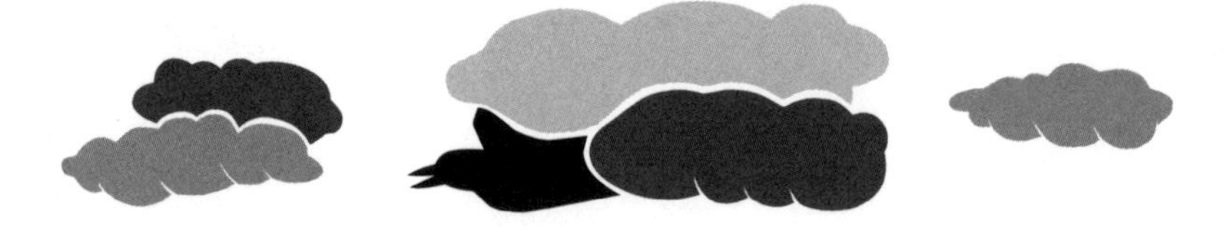

somewhere else. Occasionally, something small and very far away left a streak of white across her vision as it passed. Clouds strolled aimlessly from behind roofs and disappeared just as aimlessly behind others. The walls of the tenements were an impassable barrier. She might steal glimpses into their living rooms through the gaps in their curtains, but she had no idea whether the people she saw inside were as trapped as her, or whether they could leave their tiny rooms and go into … well, she didn't know *what*, really. More tiny rooms, perhaps, with different televisions showing programs with different theme tunes. Or maybe each room backed onto a cemetery of its own. Perhaps it was Magrit's failing that she had never found the entrance to *her* room, with *her* television.

In her mind, Magrit saw a whole world filled with

rooms attached to cemeteries attached to more rooms attached to a whole new set of cemeteries, stretching into as deep an infinity as her mind could understand: everyone in the whole world with a television and a window and a pair of curtains of their very own and a whole mountain of rubbish to eat and a Master Puppet to sit on a church roof and look after them as they grew.

Magrit wondered if all the other Master Puppets were as grumpy and sarcastic as hers, and whether everyone in the world made Master Puppets to reflect their own personalities. Maybe hers was horrible because *she* was horrible. Maybe if she was nicer, he would be too.

Magrit spat out her stick of grass and wiped her mouth. What if nobody *made* Master Puppets? What if Master Puppets lived first as thoughts that circled the minds of children until bodies were made to house them? Perhaps the people in the surrounding apartments were simply waiting for the right Master Puppet to come along and show them what body to build.

Magrit didn't know, and it had never bothered her before. She had built Master Puppet from her imagination and what she had learned from the skeletons she had discovered in the crypts. Without that knowledge, what Master Puppets were being built in the world outside the windows? What shapes were they taking? Whose voices did they use? Magrit had never considered such questions before.

"You've never had someone else to look after before," said a voice in her head. It wasn't Magrit's voice, or Master Puppet's, but something lighter, higher pitched, as if a mind had measured the two tones and picked a spot halfway between them. Magrit's eyes opened wide.

"Who are you?" she asked.

"Don't you recognise me?"

"No." Magrit glanced around in panic. "I don't know you. *Who are you?*"

"I've been here for a long time. Longer than you, my girl."

"No, you haven't!"

The new voice smiled inside her mind. "Just because you can't see me, or hear me, doesn't mean I'm not here."

"Then …" Magrit paused. The voice was opening up new questions, and she didn't know which one to ask first. "Why … why can I hear you now?"

"Oh, good question. Perhaps it's because you've never doubted your past before. Or perhaps it's because changes are coming, and you no longer believe your Master Puppet can protect you."

"That's not true!"

"Well, I guess it's all just a mystery."

Then the new voice was gone, and no matter how

much Magrit demanded it come back and tell her what it meant, it was silent.

Magrit stood, and looked all around her, but the cemetery was as it always was: quiet, peaceful and vacant. She could see Master Puppet in the distance, contemplating his tiny domain. Her gaze lingered on the chapel, moved almost of its own accord along the wall towards the rear corner, then jumped away to land on the nearby building as if burned. The blank windows that formed the walls of her world looked back at her with disinterest. Overhead, something grey fluttered out from behind a building, then fell across her vision until it landed on the other side of the cemetery. An empty bag, Magrit guessed, promising riches but giving nothing.

Magrit laid her head back down. The sun was warm and mild. Bugrat snored gently at her feet. The grass spread out around her like a warm blanket, hiding her from view and muffling the sounds of the insects and tiny mammals that occupied the grounds. She had imagined the voice, she decided. Imagined it, or made it up to keep herself awake. Within seconds she was asleep, and dreaming of countless Master Puppets, enfolding her in bony, loving hugs.

+X+

ONCE BUGRAT HAD TAKEN ONE step he wanted to take another, and another, and as many as he could manage before he fell over. In no time at all he was toddling about the cemetery as fast as his chubby legs could carry him. By the time summer began to warm the ground and fill the upper windows of the building with reflected light, Magrit had to scurry to keep up.

Now he could walk, it seemed that all he wanted

to do was step off the edge of things, or clamber up the crumbling crypt walls to a point where it was too high for him to get down, or run and trip and run and trip and run and trip until his pudgy knees were a mess of scabs and she had to croon made-up lullabies to stop him crying.

Magrit invented new games to teach him the proper way to walk around the cemetery: Chase-and-Catch around the headstones and Upsey-Overs along the cracked and ruptured footpaths. She found a punctured football that was too flat to roll properly but bumbled and flolloped this way and that and brought a torrent of giggles from Bugrat as he chased it. Soon, all the private nooks and crannies and corners that she had thought were hers alone now belonged to both of them.

There was no stopping Bugrat. He covered the ground in a determined waddle, his desire for exploration rewarded with a squeal of joy every time he discovered something new. Magrit followed along behind him, laughing with each revelation, smothering him in hugs with every shared experience, and only once holding him back and refusing entry to a part of the grounds.

In the entire cemetery, the corner behind the chapel was the only place Magrit would not enter. It was a triangle of high grass maybe twenty steps in every direction: the rear of the chapel formed one side of the triangle; two buildings met to form the other two sides. A short iron fence joined the chapel wall to the buildings, except for a gap where a gate had once stood. Now it lay flat on the ground, its rotting wood providing a soft warning to go no further.

Magrit would never do so. She didn't like the corner. It wasn't darker than any other spot in the cemetery, or colder, and the grass that grew wild and high there was no different to the grass that she enjoyed running through in all the other quarters. Still, there was something about this tiny area that caused dark clouds of worry and fear to gather in Magrit's mind.

Late at night, her dreams turned towards this part of the graveyard and sent her stumbling through the tall grass, her skin so hot she feared she might set the dry blades alight, until she screamed aloud and woke up, and spent the hours until dawn clutching her ragged blanket and vowing never to set foot inside that horrid triangle of empty ground.

So she never squeezed through the gap during daylight hours and explored it. She simply turned her mind away and pretended it didn't exist.

Magrit was so good at forgetting about the corner that when she entered the crypt to wake Bugrat from his afternoon nap one day and found an empty nest of blanket scraps instead of a sleeping child, she did not even consider the idea that he might go there. She searched everywhere else, her footsteps growing ever quicker as he declined to appear in section after section of the cemetery.

Bugrat wasn't in the rotten vault, where all the walls had fallen in on each other and buried the stone sarcophagus at its centre, and where she sometimes played Hide-and-Find with him after eating. He wasn't sitting between the tangled tomato plants where Magrit and he rested when it was hot, lying on their tummies in the shade and sucking the juice and seeds out of the fruits while they still hung on the branches. And he wasn't running around the bag maze, skipping through the ranks of heavy unbroken garbage bags that Magrit had laid out ready to open and rummage through.

By this time, Magrit was running from corner to corner and back again, searching under every headstone and through every head-high clump of grass, calling his name in a strangled, high-pitched whisper, afraid to shout too loudly in case she caught the attention of those in the apartments around her.

"You're looking in the wrong places." The new voice was back, teasing, laughing. Magrit turned in a circle, her eyes wide in panic.

"Where are you? Where is he?"

"You'll find him when you find yourself," the voice said, and faded away.

"What do you mean? Where is he?"

But the voice was gone, and Bugrat was nowhere to be seen. And no matter how often she stopped and stood still, and bent her head just so, to try to catch a sound that didn't belong and might lead her to him, he was nowhere to be heard either.

The shadows chased her across the cemetery, growing longer and longer as the sun fell behind the surrounding buildings, drowning their craggy edges in deep black until they resembled the smooth, rounded headstones they guarded. Finally, though she didn't want to confess to having lost him, she stood before the chapel and peered up to where Master Puppet sat above her.

"Can you help me?" she asked.

"Can you help me find Bugrat?"

Master Puppet stayed silent for the longest time. Magrit bit her lip. He had heard her question. He was just deciding which jibe would make her feel worst, which tone of voice would cut her feelings into the smallest pieces. Magrit felt her face tighten. She wasn't going to cry, she decided. She was responsible. She was grown up. Not grown up like Master Puppet, but a different kind of grown up. One that didn't cry in the face of Master Puppet.

Then he spoke, and for half a second she didn't know *what* to think. "Certainly," he said, in his politest, most caring voice. "I know exactly where he is."

"You do?"

"Oh, yes."

Magrit folded her hands in her lap and made sure to use her absolutely best manners. "Would you be so kind as to tell me where?" she asked.

"Of course," Master Puppet replied. "I saw him run

down the side of my chapel an hour ago. He's been playing behind me since then."

Rivers of cold ran through Magrit's body. Goosebumps tickled her arms and chest, and her face and neck grew hot and spiky like she had been rubbing them with sharp grass.

"He is where?"

Master Puppet's voice had not changed, but now it was a fearful and terrible thing. "He's playing behind us. Behind the chapel. You'll have to go and get him."

"But … I can't." Magrit was caught in a sudden wave of terror. She wanted to run away, to hide at the bottom of the deepest, darkest corner of the graveyard, to put her hands over her eyes and pull rubbish over herself until nobody could ever find her again. Anywhere, anywhere but the corner that filled her heart with so much cold water. But her legs wouldn't move, and all she could do was look from side to side and let tears bubble up and trickle down her cheeks. She wasn't grown up any more, and Master Puppet could see her cry as much as he wanted, so long as he changed his answer. "I can't."

"You have to." He wasn't going to let her back out; Magrit knew that. She was trapped between her fear and his disdain. Now she understood why he had been so nice. He didn't have to shout at her or say nasty things in his superior grown-up voice. This was punishment enough. "If you want him back, you'll have to go and get him."

"Please." She bounced up and down. Energy filled her, but had nowhere to go, no way to escape. "Please don't make me."

"Why?" And Master Puppet said the words she didn't want to hear, and asked her the question she never, ever wanted to think about. "What are you afraid of?"

"I don't know!" she cried. At last, her legs moved. Her knees bent and lowered her to the cold concrete path, snuffling tears and runny snot, and blubbing out all the distress and fear she couldn't keep inside any longer.

Master Puppet waited until she was finished, until her sobbing ran down towards silence. Then his voice was inside her head, warm and slithery like an evil, smiling lizard. "You'll have to go," he said. "You don't know if he'll come out by himself." His voice oozed with I-told-you-so smugness as he exposed her fear and gave it words. "Maybe he'll stay there forever. He might never come out. And then where will you be?

ALL ALONE again.

Is that what you want? To be by yourself, with nobody to love you or remember you when you're gone?" His voice slid around her denials, scraping at her thoughts with sharp, sharp nails. When she could stand it no longer she jumped up.

"All right!" she snapped, as she rubbed the wetness from her face with a sleeve. "Leave me alone."

"I'm sorry," Master Puppet said in his polite, friendly voice. "I was helping you, as you requested. I apologise if that upsets you."

Magrit's eyes were hot. She glared up at her tormentor. "I hate you."

"Well, then," he replied. "You'll *really* want to go and get your little friend back, won't you?"

Magrit could think of nothing more to say. All she could do was stamp one foot, turn her back and stomp around the corner of the chapel, hoping that all the anger inside her would give her the power to march right up to Bugrat and pull him out before whatever caused her so much dread could find her.

Her rage flew away as soon as she turned the bend and fear slipped in where it had been. Soon, she was sneaking along, gripping the stone wall with stiff fingers, the gap leading to the hidden garden getting closer, and closer, like a giant mouth just waiting to bite and chew and swallow her up.

The walls of the chapel seemed to shrink as they approached the forbidden quadrant. Magrit kept her face pressed against them, afraid to look away in case the walls deserted her and gave her nothing to cling onto. The smooth surface near the front door gave way to pitted and ridged stones, which threw tiny shadows across themselves so that it appeared a million tiny eyes were observing her as she crept closer. Grass, tall and stiff, whispered strange truths as the wind stirred through it. The rotting metal fence leered at her with broken palings, the rusted gate hinges clicked in the breeze. The wall of the chapel ran out, until she found herself reluctantly wrapping her fingertips around its far edge, their white tips out of sight around the bend. She wanted to tilt her head to peek beyond the pitted grey stone, but there was no strength in her neck to do so.

"Bugrat," she whispered, hoping without hope that he might be right next to her, only just out of sight, and would come toddling around the corner in answer to her voice. "Bugrat."

Bugrat did not come. Magrit risked a louder call. "Bugrat. Bugrat!"

And still she was alone, the side of her face pressed hard into the stone wall, eyes squeezed into squinty slits so she didn't have to see the awful green and brown space before her. Her legs gave way, and she kneeled on her hands and knees, bunching her body into a ball so she took up the smallest amount of space possible.

Slowly, she reached out one hand and placed it on the grass beyond the rear of the chapel.

Nothing happened.

Magrit opened one eye and examined her hand. It was where it always was: a thin, white, five-legged spider at the end of her wrist. She wriggled her fingers, feeling the grass tickle them. Nothing bit her or stung her exposed skin. Nobody leaned out of a nearby window to yell "Hey, you!" and bring her world to a standstill. No monsters appeared before her. Magrit swallowed and glanced around, feeling just the tiniest bit silly. She drew her hand back in, expecting the sky to fall in upon her. When nothing happened she dropped back against the stone wall and sat upright.

There was nothing to fear. She knew it. She could see the grassed area if she leaned forwards and tilted her head in the right direction. It looked just like any other neglected corner of the cemetery: gritty brown walls surrounding a patch of yellow grass, with only the curtains inside the windows lending any colour at all. Small noises skittered through the grass stalks, and the weak sunlight bounced back and forth between the windowpanes until it seemed to shine from every direction at once. Whatever she was afraid of was inside her, not in this pathetic, empty angle of brick and stone.

Bugrat was in there somewhere. She needed to find him and bring him home before the night grew too deep and she risked losing him until morning. She dragged herself to her feet, and stared at the thin gap between safety and the terrifying unknown beyond.

"I can do this," she said. "I can."

She shut her eyes and closed out the thoughts that swirled inside her head. She took one deep breath, and another, then stepped away from the safety of the wall and into the open space beyond.

And collapsed.

+X+

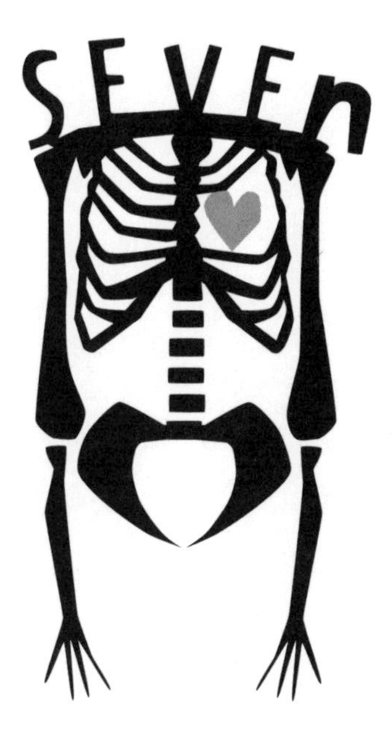

IT TOOK MAGRIT A LONG time to wake up. There was a voice in her head, one she didn't recognise. It was calling her name, over and over, as if searching for her among the long grass.

Magrit opened her eyes. The sun had disappeared behind the buildings, and the shadows were crawling down the walls exactly the way they did just before night embraced the graveyard. She covered her ears with her hands, but the voice didn't go away. It wasn't Master Puppet. It wasn't the hum of the surrounding buildings, drawn up into a single voice to finally talk to her directly. It sounded like a girl, with a voice just like Magrit's but slightly deeper, slightly stronger and more confident in its own strength.

Her words echoed around inside Magrit's skull, making her want to cry out, to call "Here, Mummy!" and wave her hands until someone swept her up into a warm hug and carried her away to safety and love and things she couldn't name but suddenly wanted more than anything else in the world. Magrit gasped as the pain of wanting pushed against the walls of her heart. The stranger's words became clear, and all of Magrit's desires melted away, leaving her body hollow and cold.

She recognised the voice. It was the same one that had taunted her while she lay dreaming in the grass. And it was inside her head.

"Who are you?" Magrit whispered. As soon as she said it, the voice stopped calling.

"You know who I am," it replied.

"Are you ..." For a second she didn't know who it might be, so she said the only name for whom she could not find a voice. "Are you Bugrat?"

"No." The voice laughed, soft and sad. "He won't have a voice until he has someone to speak to."

"What do you mean?" Magrit should have been angry, but she found herself fearful of the voice's answer.

"You know what I mean."

"No, I don't."

"Yes, you do." The voice was quiet for long seconds, then said more quietly, "Deep down. Deep down, you know."

"No." Magrit shook her head, hoping she could knock the stranger loose. "*Who* are you?"

"Yes," a new voice intruded. Master Puppet's voice: strident, demanding, superior. "Please. Tell me exactly who it is."

The voice ignored him. "You have to stop hiding,"

it said. "You have to stop pretending that this is all forever."

"I *insist* that I be told who this person is!" Magrit could hear the journey Master Puppet's voice was taking. She knew where it would end up, in a place where he was screaming at her in rage, and she was in tears and wondering what on earth she had done wrong.

"She says I have to stop hiding. She says–"

"She? *She?* I hear no she!"

"He can't really hear me," the girl's voice whispered in Magrit's ear. "He just knows he doesn't want you talking to anyone else."

"Please," Magrit sobbed. "I just want Bugrat."

"He's over there," the girl whispered, and then said no more.

Magrit turned her attention outwards. She was lying full-length inside the forbidden quarter. Something was moving in the scattered clumps of grass to the rear corner. Magrit felt her heart thump against her ribs. Her breath came out in tiny spurts. All she wanted was to throw herself back round the corner of the chapel and run far, far away from whatever terrible thing was causing the grass to shake and shiver. Instead, she forced herself up until she was on her knees. Carefully, one terrified hand after another, she crawled towards the source of her fear.

It was Bugrat, of course. She had known it, from the rustling movement she could hear through the grass as she approached, and the way the girl in her head had directed her towards him. She didn't understand how the voice knew where he was, but that didn't matter. After all, Master Puppet knew things she didn't, and she had built him with her own hands. But it wasn't important, not right then, because there was Bugrat, and he was safe and happy.

Magrit scooted through the grass, ready to smother him in hugs and kisses, and run back with him to where they could both be out of harm's way, and she could teach him never to come back to this corner of the cemetery ever again.

"Bugrat!" she called, the joy in her voice causing small, invisible things in the grass to scuttle out of her way. Bugrat looked up, saw her and waved a chubby, dirt-filled fist in greeting. Magrit quickened her step. All she wanted to do was take hold of him and make her escape. She was almost upon him when she looked over his shoulder and saw what he was doing.

He had cleared away the rubbish bags that littered the space in which he sat. He had trampled the grass until it was flat and empty. He had dug into the dirt with his plump little fingers, burrowing down until he uncovered the ground in a circle perhaps three times his length in diameter. And there he sat, patting his hands against the dirt, tapping out a clumsy rhythm with his fists against the ground. Magrit might have recognised the tunes she sang to him as he fell asleep at night, mixed up together and backwards and upside down and inside out, if she wasn't gawking with wide eyes at the thing Bugrat had uncovered.

The cemetery was full of dead people. It had always been that way, since long before Magrit had come to live there. They gave her their clothes to wear. They let her sleep in their buildings. Their graves provided flowers to splash colour through the grass. Their headstones were islands among the rubbish piles. They volunteered their bones to make Master Puppet. Magrit was comfortable with the dead. They did not sadden her, or revolt her, or scare her. She was used to seeing them in every stage of their afterlife. Skin and bones and dirt in the gaps and crevices did not, in her opinion, mean a dead person was a *bad* person. They were simply part of her world, to be treated with respect.

Bugrat had found a skeleton, and it scared Magrit silly.

It was a small skeleton, obviously a child, curled up on its side as if sleeping, with its legs drawn up towards its chest and arms folded up as if hugging a non-existent teddy bear. It wore a grey smock that covered everything but one arm and its skull, which was tucked into its chest as if the child was trying to keep warm on a cold night. It was hard for Magrit to tell, but it *might* have been about her height and age. A child nearly ten years old: undersized for its age, its bones warped and bent. Magrit knew, without knowing quite *how* she knew, that it was a girl.

She peered from left to right in panic. She could see no headstone lying in the grass, no outline of a path or grave boundary to show that the dead child belonged to anybody who cared. It was simply *there*, with Bugrat sitting next to it. He looked up at Magrit with a proud smile on his muddy face as if he had done something very clever and was waiting for her to tell him how wonderful he was. Magrit couldn't speak. She couldn't tear her eyes away from the bones.

It was *this* skeleton that had made her so afraid to come to this part of the cemetery for so long. She was terrified just looking at it. Her feet had lost all feeling. They refused to turn her around and carry her away. She didn't know why she was so frightened, didn't know why this poor child, cold and abandoned and forgotten, could fill her bones with ice and freeze her to the spot. But it did. It did, and Magrit wanted to beg it to stop, to tell it she was sorry, even though she didn't know what she was sorry for.

Master Puppet was calling her, asking, "What is it? What have you found? Magrit, what have you found?" in his worried voice, over and over again. His voice was dull, muted, as if she heard it through ears full of clotted dirt.

And just when she thought she would never be able to move again, that time and earth and the heaviness of her limbs would keep her rooted to this spot forevermore, she stared down into the skull's eye sockets, and heard the mystery girl's voice inside her head again, rising out of the whistling wind of time, loud and clear.

"Told you I was here," she said.

Just like that, fire ran through Magrit's limbs, warming them into action. She swept Bugrat into her arms and took off, running blindly through the long grass. She slipped past the gap between the corner of the chapel and the wall, scraping her back across the rough stone and crying out as she felt it bite into her skin. Then she was out, into the centre of the cemetery, away, away, away as far as she could get before the strength left her and she fell to her hands and knees. She dropped Bugrat onto a clump of flowers and hugged herself tight as she cried and cried and cried.

And all the time she did so, the girl's voice stayed

quiet, and so did Bugrat and Master Puppet, so silent and still that it was a long time before Magrit realised that the whole world had fallen silent. The birds no longer twittered and tweeted as they swooped to pluck soundless insects from the air. The murmur and hum that always emanated from the surrounding buildings, so prevalent that she never really noticed, was painful in its absence.

"Hello?" Magrit cried out. "Hello?" But the only voice inside her head was her own.

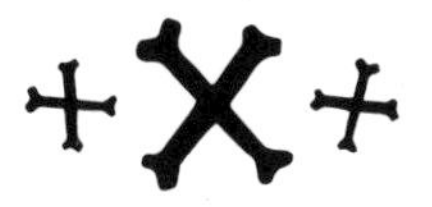

SHE CAME BACK TO HER senses after a long time. In the tiniest portions, the sounds of the world began to leak back into her head. Magrit kneeled with her forehead against the wall of the chapel and let the sound fill her up. Night covered the graveyard. By the time she found the strength to pick Bugrat up and wash him in a nearby font, it was almost completely dark. She carried him inside the crypt farthest from

Master Puppet's perch. There she changed him into a fresh, dry set of clothes that were barely musty at all and watched him curl up into a nest of rags and fall asleep. When she was sure he wasn't going to wake, she dragged herself outside and shuffled over to confront Master Puppet.

"Why did you do that?" she asked. He did not look at her.

"Do what?" he replied. "Point out where your toy was? Let you discover for yourself how dangerous the course you're taking is? Give you the chance to realise what a mistake this child continues to be?"

"He's not a mistake! He's my–"

"Your what? Your brother? Your friend? Your baby?" Magrit heard the sneer in his voice. She understood how stupid he thought she was, how utterly stupid and small and incapable.

"All of them!" she screamed. "He's all of them!"

"He is your *disaster*," Master Puppet said in a cold, calm voice. "He is your undoing.

HE IS THE RUIN OF EVERYTHING WE HAVE BUILT TOGETHER, YOU AND I.

When it happens, when it goes horribly wrong and there is no way to put things back together again, it will be your fault."

"*My* fault? What about you?"

"I have had nothing to do with it."

"That's what I mean! You're supposed to help me. You're supposed to make things better–"

"I am *supposed* to do nothing," he said. "I *choose* to offer you guidance …"

Magrit scrunched her face up. "The girl's voice is right about you," she muttered. The air between her and Master Puppet grew very cold.

"What," he said in a low, dangerous tone, "girl's voice?"

Magrit narrowed her eyes. "I'm not going to tell you."

"You must!" Master Puppet was angry now, as angry as she had ever seen him. "You must tell me now!"

"No, I don't think I will."

"Don't be so stupid–"

There was a rock in Magrit's hand. She did not know how it got there or where it came from. But there it was and, without a second thought, she threw it at Master Puppet. It struck him on the head and whirled away. Master Puppet's face swung towards her. She saw his wide eye sockets and his jaw dropping agape, as if he was shocked to his empty heart at what she had done. Then, before she could open her mouth to speak, to apologise or tell him it was what he deserved for being so mean, before she could even make up her mind which one was the right thing to say and which one she meant, he fell backwards. She watched in horror as he slid down the angled roof away from her and disappeared over the edge. She heard him fall to the ground at the far side of the building, a clatter of bones like dry rain that went on for far too long and then was far, far too silent.

"Master Puppet?" she whispered, and again, when he did not answer, "Master Puppet?"

But Master Puppet had nothing to say and, for the first time since she had built him, Magrit could not see his hunched body outlined against the surrounding apartments. She could not bear to look at the hole in the air where he had been. She ran to the corner of the chapel in a panic, and found a tangle of bones and sticks in the middle of the grass.

"Master Puppet?"

Somewhere, in the back of her heart, Magrit had always been afraid that Master Puppet's voice was only *her* voice, bouncing back to her off the inside of his round, empty skull; that all she heard when he spoke was the girl she might grow up to be, talking at her through his mouth and her imagination. She had become accustomed to pretending that Master Puppet was a real person, with real feelings and thoughts and words and opinions. When she glanced through the door of the crypt and saw him perched atop his chapel like a scarecrow made from spare parts and cobwebs, rattling in the wind, it was easy to think of him as something she had invented to stop her feeling quite so lonely. At those times, Magrit had to close her eyes against the fear that he was nothing more than a yellowed, jangling mirror that showed the inside of her mind to her. No. Master Puppet was real, and so his *questions* were real. And his questions made her cold and scared and lonely all over again.

Now the mound of bones was silent. Magrit spied his skull away to the left, upside down and separated from his spine. Scraps of cloth that once tied arms and legs together fluttered in the breeze, and sticks that had held ribs apart, or had taken the place of bones she could not find or could not fit together properly, now lay broken and snapped like an overturned bird's nest.

"Master Puppet?"

She snuck to within arm's reach of the pile that had once been her friend, expecting to hear his voice boom inside her head, scolding her for breaking him and demanding he be put back together. There was a space in her mind where he should be, and all she could sense was the emptiness of him not being there.

Magrit reached a shaking hand towards his skull. His jaw was not attached, she could see, now she was close. It had bounced away somewhere and she could not spy it. Perhaps that was why he did not speak. Maybe he was trying to call to her, and the wind that rushed through her mind was the sound of him not being able to form words properly. Her fingers brushed the round cold curve of his skull and she knew her lie for what it was.

Master Puppet only existed because she had made him, with her hands and her determination and her mind. These cold, yellowed bones were not the sum of his existence. That sum existed inside *her*, along with his voice and his knowledge and his guidance. Without him she was just a lost child. Without her, without her need for him to exist as a real, solid thing, he was nothing at all.

"My voice," she breathed, as the skull's empty eye sockets looked at her with no trace of emotion. "My voice all along."

And then there *was* a sound inside her head. But it was not Master Puppet. It was the other voice: the new one, the smirking, superior girl from the place beyond the chapel walls.

"You've done it now," she said. "You've broken him well and proper."

"Shut up." Magrit cradled the skull in her arms. "Shut up."

"You'll never put him back together."

"Shut up." She was crying now, big tears that burned her eyes and made her nose itch. "You're not real," she snapped, aflame with her new knowledge. "You're just a voice inside my head, like … like …" Try as she might, she still could not say his name, could not acknowledge out loud what she knew in her heart.

"Oh, that I am," the girl's voice admitted. "That and more."

"Oh, be quiet, you *stupid* girl!" And with those words, the spell of the girl's voice was broken. Because it was Magrit who had barked the words, but it was Master Puppet's voice she had used. The girl fell silent, and Magrit rocked back and forth, clutching the bony globe to her chest. "I'm sorry," she told his absence. "I'm sorry. I'm sorry. I'm sorry."

"You can't do it," the girl's voice said softly, almost apologetically. "You can't do it on your own."

"I can so," Magrit whispered. "I can … I can …"

She stopped, her attention drawn into the gap between the chapel and the wall, as if finally listening to what the voice was saying, not with her words, but with the spaces in between them, where a different meaning was revealed.

"Thank you," Magrit said at last. There was a pause, and the dead girl replied.

"You're welcome."

+X+

THE FOLLOWING MORNING, MAGRIT WAS up before the sun, ready to go back to the chapel and rebuild her friend. Perhaps she could do it by herself, given enough time and a large slice of luck, but the skeleton girl had told her something important. That she didn't *have* to do it alone. She had Bugrat. And she had the skeleton girl and the skeleton girl's voice. If she could build a friend who loved her and looked after her, no matter how mean and superior he might behave, then what would he be like if Bugrat helped? And the girl? Would the new Master Puppet love and look after Bugrat as well, once there was a part of his skeleton that would always carry his touch? Would he be inside the little boy's head, like he was in hers, mirroring Bugrat's dreams and fears and need for protection. Or would that remain Magrit's role alone? Magrit did not know. All she could do was try, and hope some of the boy's happiness and laughter might be caught up inside the nest of bones and twigs as they worked.

Bugrat was still sleeping. She shook him awake and, as he rubbed his eyes and tried to turn over, she pulled him out of his nest and bundled him through the door and into the open air. He began to complain, his face scrunched up in annoyance. Magrit fretted that he would stay like this and infect Master Puppet with his baby-like crankiness. She calmed him with a fresh tomato and a short dance together, then whisked him away to where Master Puppet lay. She located Master Puppet's skull first, where she had laid it carefully the night before. She picked it up and, stroking it like she did Bugrat's face when he was struggling for sleep, set her companion the task of gathering the scattered bones.

Bugrat took to it with glee, rummaging through the grass like the most determined of treasure hunters. He picked out finger bones and toe bones and knee bones and arm bones. Soon enough he found the missing jaw, which he held above his head like a flag while he marched round and round in circles. They ran out of bones to find, and sat next to each other with the pile before them, placing them in the rough semblance of a person.

Then they set to work. Bugrat chose each bone in its turn. Magrit sorted and placed them, arranging and rearranging, checking the pattern against her own skinny frame to make sure she could twist and turn and click them into each other like a real body.

"It's not enough," she said, eyeing the tattered remains. "There's so much missing. He'll fall apart again." She sank to her knees and put her head in her hands. "I've killed him."

"Not yet," the girl's voice sounded in her mind. "You've got one source of bones you haven't considered."

"Where?"

"Bugrat."

"No! You can't have his bones."

"Don't be stupid."

"Don't call me that!" Magrit stood up, fists clenched. "You're just like … just like …" She glanced down at Master Puppet's inanimate skeleton.

"Oh, I'm better than him," the voice replied. "I know Bugrat's going to work it out before you, and I give my bones up because I want to."

"What? No!"

Before Magrit could react, Bugrat was on his way, toddling past her and disappearing into the corner behind the chapel.

"No!" She ran after him, then stopped at the fence line. She couldn't bring herself to go further. Instead, she swayed on the spot, hopping from one foot to the other in unbearable tension, hissing, "Please, please, please ..." like a prayer, over and over and over.

He returned, a dozen or more bones in his arms. Magrit retreated before him as he walked purposefully back to Master Puppet and dropped them at the skeleton's feet. "But these are ..."

"A donation. Use them wisely," the girl said.

"These are your bones."

"They are ours," the girl replied. "To use as we see fit. Now use them and make him whole."

"Why?" Magrit asked. "Why are you helping? You don't even like him."

"You don't have to like somebody to love them."

"You ... love him?"

The girl laughed. "YOU do. And I want what's best for you. So. Use the bones. Reassemble your friend. Then let us see whether it really is what's best for you."

"But ... what about you?"

"I'll be fine," the voice replied. "I've lost more than this and survived. In my own way."

"Your own way?"

"Just use the bones."

Without stopping to think, Magrit began to pick up bones and fit them into the design she had laid out before her. She dispatched her eager assistant to pull up strands of grass for her to twine into cords, and search through the tangled vines that adorned the nearby buildings to tear down exactly the right one to coil and bend and knot, and rummage about in their nests for rags of just the right length to tie everything together.

The sun rose towards noon and then fell into the afternoon. With lots of mistakes and changes and giggles and tears of frustration and yelps of triumph, with hugs and grunts and concentration and practice, they built themselves a skeleton.

It didn't look much like a real skeleton. There weren't enough ribs and a lot of what it *did* have were sticks. It had not quite as many toes as it could have and some of its fingers were made from broken cutlery that Magrit bent into shape. There was a tin can in the middle of its spine and most of its teeth were missing. But that was what had made Master Puppet who he was: if Magrit wanted a simple skeleton, she could have picked one from the graves around her. What she needed was *Master Puppet*.

Master Puppet, she understood now, had always been

more than just bones and advice. He was a frame upon which she hung her deepest thoughts, and now it was a frame for thoughts that she and Bugrat were rebuilding. And the frame they built had a skull, with holes for its eyes and a jaw that opened and shut with the breeze, like Master Puppet's did. It had two legs, and two arms – more or less – and a sort of lap that reminded her of the bony cradle into which she had crawled when she was smaller and in need of comfort. And it was, for as much as she wished it to be, her Master Puppet, only now it was hers and Bugrat's and the skeleton girl's, all wrapped together like a conversation where each of them finished the other's sentences. And, she hoped, he would be all the better for it. All she needed to do was lean him against the wall of the chapel and wait for him to speak, and they could be a family again.

With Bugrat helping as much as a one year old could, she picked Master Puppet up and together they propped him just so against the wall, with his hands in his lap and his skull resting gently against the stone.

Then they sat down like the quietest, politest children in the world, and waited.

And waited.

And waited.

After a while Bugrat crawled into her lap and snuggled down. She positioned her hands around him and tried not to think of just how much she looked like Master Puppet.

The sky was lowering all around them. Shadows were creeping down the bricks towards the grass. Magrit peeked up at the sky and saw the empty roof above them.

"Of course!" She shook Bugrat awake. "The roof," she cried. "The roof!"

Master Puppet lived on the roof, where he could look across the cemetery and make sure everything was in its place, and where he could protect Magrit all day and all night like the guardian she needed him to be. It was his job and his purpose. Until he was at that high point, until he was in his appointed place, he was not Master Puppet. He was just a jigsaw puzzle with ambition.

It took until the shadows had crept over the whole cemetery for Magrit to climb the chapel wall and drag Master Puppet's body up with her. Six times he caught on rough stones, or the edge of the gutter, or on vines or branches that grew through the windows and along the walls, and dropped part of himself back down onto the grass. Six times she found a spot to wedge him into and clambered down to recover the rogue bone and fit it back into him before she continued. She stuck to it and, while Bugrat played clapping games with himself, she hauled him to the front of the building. She arranged his legs on either side of the big cross that stood at its apex and draped his arms over the crossbar like she had done once before. Carefully, she took her hands away so that he was, once again, sitting by himself. As the shadows met and the darkness of the night descended, she positioned his skull so he gazed out over the graveyard beneath them. She held her breath, and waited.

Perhaps it didn't take as long as it felt, because it felt like forever and ever, but after the longest time there was a sound inside her mind like someone not quite knowing what to say, like *her* not quite knowing what to say to herself. Then Master Puppet's voice, tender and scratchy like he had a sore throat, came whispering towards her.

"AND HOW..."

he said, his voice quiet like he was embarrassed and wary and thankful all at the same time. Magrit caught a tiny breath in her throat: it was him, just like she had hoped, only more than that, she heard the high, feathery tendrils of the skeleton girl's voice, playing around his like a breeze.

"YOU CAN GET DOWN IF YOU WANT TO. THE DARK IS NO PROBLEM FOR YOU."

Magrit glanced over the edge of the roof. She saw a dim shape in the dark, just about where she imagined Bugrat might be if he grew bored with waiting and snuggled down to sleep. She saw the lights coming on in the windows around her, as the people who lived behind the curtains turned on televisions to keep them company. She felt Master Puppet within her thoughts, warm and quietly happy and, most important of all, *there*. She squirmed closer to him, wrapped his arm over her shoulder and tucked her head into the bony angles of his lap, settled herself onto the cold tiles and made sure she wouldn't slip.

"I'm not going to leave," she said.

MASTER PUPPET WAS BACK AND all was as it should be. Or, if it wasn't *exactly* as it should be, it was as close as it was likely to get. His voice wasn't quite as Magrit remembered. It was scratchier and less certain. The skeleton girl's bones chimed differently in the wind, so that he sounded smaller and higher pitched. And he no longer surveyed the cemetery with the same air of confidence as he once had, but rather more as if he was afraid of what he might view and was bracing himself against it. He was back on his perch where he belonged, to reassure Magrit with the shape of his silhouette against the blank red bricks any time she wished to glance up. And Magrit glanced up a lot, to make sure he was there, and that all the pieces she and Bugrat had used to rebuild him were attached, and he was looking out for her. But mostly just to make sure he was still there.

He spoke less often and what he did say was tinged with sadness, or at least a kind of softness, as if he was delivering bad news but did not want to hurt anybody while he did so. He often trailed away in mid-sentence and, when Bugrat came into his vision, he occasionally fell silent, as if losing interest in Magrit altogether.

"What are you doing?" she asked him once, when she saw him regarding Bugrat as he played in front of the chapel.

"I'm talking to him," Master Puppet replied.

"What do you talk to him about?"

"Oh, just bits and bobs," he said, his voice like the touch of grass against her face. "Just bits and bobs."

"What sort of bits?"

Master Puppet said nothing, but Magrit had the feeling that he was contemplating Bugrat, measuring him with much less fierceness than he had once done.

"I talk to him of the future," he said at last. "You can see a lot of it from up here."

"What …" Suddenly, Magrit was unsure which question to ask, and which answer she hoped for. "What can you see?"

"Growth," he replied.

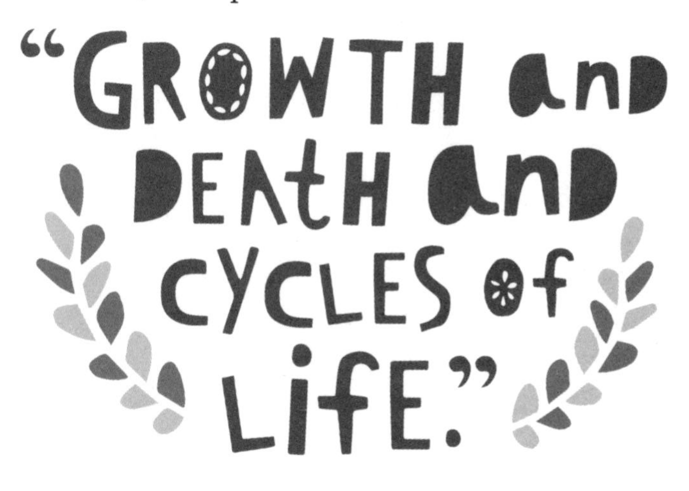

Magrit looked around her, at the grass and the graves, and the insects that flickered and fluttered about them. "You can see all that down here, if you look at it," she said.

"Yes. Yes, I'm sure you can."

At her feet, Bugrat pulled at her dress. She stooped and picked him up, hugging him tight.

"Does he …" She licked her lips. "Does he ever ask you anything?"

Inside her head, Master Puppet smiled a slow, sad smile. "No," he said. "Never. I'm afraid I'm never certain if he even hears me."

"*I* hear you. I always hear you."

"Do you?"

"Yes!"

"That's good." Magrit had the sensation of Master Puppet nodding. "That's very good."

The days rolled on and Bugrat spent hours exploring while Magrit hovered at a safe distance, letting him meander where he wished and always wondering just how much help he might require, or whether she would hear him should he ever find his voice and cry out, or if he really needed her at all now he could walk from wall to wall without falling.

And he grew into his second year and into his third and, finally, into his fourth year. Magrit, who had been nearly ten years old throughout his years of growth and who now, still nearly ten, fretted more often than she ought, and found herself talking to him more and more in a voice that sounded a little like Master Puppet and a lot like the skeleton in the grass.

Everybody was talking except Bugrat. No matter what Magrit tried, she could not persuade him to speak, to respond to her pleas with anything but burbling and silence.

"What is this?" she would ask hopefully, pointing to a familiar plant and "What's that called?" and "What is this for?" and "Why?" and "Why?" and "Why?" over and over again, but the only thing she received in reply were hugs and kisses and silent giggles.

Magrit had never taught anybody before. She didn't know how to make someone sit and listen and believe that she was the only one who knew the *real* truth about things.

"Why are they called headstones?" she would ask, pointing to the slabs of stone that lay facedown among the grass. Bugrat had no words to tell her "Because they are." And, because jumping from stone to stone was what Magrit and Bugrat used them for, she changed their name to jumpstones, and jumpstones they became.

"What are they?" she asked of the stars that flickered beyond the edges of the surrounding roofs when the night sky cleared and the smog dissipated. And because he would not answer, she filled his silence with explanations.

"Windows," she said. "Windows in the sky. And that blackness, all around them? It's a garden, where little boys and girls can play safely." She gazed up at the infinite night and her voice took on a wistful tone. "No walls to hold them in, no walls at all. Nothing to stop them from playing wherever they want. No need to fear the stars and worry about who might look out of them." And then she turned him away and left the stars and the open sky to their business.

The real windows, on the other hand, were *her* business. Bugrat was fascinated by the shining squares of light, and she spent far too often warning him away from them. No sooner did Magrit take her eyes off him than he was scooting through the grass, running from the centre of the cemetery to the walls of the building with his arms outstretched.

"What are you doing?" she asked, pulling on his arm yet again, relying on her greater weight to drag him away. Bugrat struggled, then fell back and allowed her to carry him away, back into the safety of the brambles and the deep, comfortable shadows.

"You must never touch them," she cautioned him as she deposited him on the flattened grass in front of the chapel, bending down so that she could hold his face in her hands while she spoke. "Never, ever, ever."

"Why not?" someone always asked. Not Bugrat. Bugrat never asked why. Instead it was the girl's voice, slipping in between the gaps in Magrit's concentration like a snake between stones in a wall. "What harm is there?"

"You know why," Magrit would tell her. "You know what it would mean."

"I do. I do," the girl's voice agreed.

And Magrit would ignore her, then, and turn her attention back to her ward. Because Bugrat never asked why and so she never had to tell him: they never touched the window because it was the *rule*. That was all. It was the rule. It kept them safe. It must simply never be done.

So the days passed. Magrit was happy. The slow, temporary warmth of summer drew the chill from the stones and made the dry grass hiss as they pushed through it, and warmed the water they splashed on their faces in the morning. Magrit knew that this was the best, the happiest, the most complete, that she had felt in her entire life.

And then, one cooling autumn day, when Bugrat was nearly four and a half and Magrit was still nearly ten, she woke and realised that, for the first time since she discovered the skeleton in the grass, the world around her was completely soundless. She blinked and raised her hands to rub at her ears in surprise. There was always *some* background noise, even in the heart of the cemetery, even buried under her nest of rags in the great stone crypt in which she slept. Insects ticked and chirruped. Rats scuttled. Breezes swished the grass and rattled the wires in Master Puppet's bones. Stone walls heated and cooled and whispered stories to her about the lives they contained within their depths. Now, again, she was surrounded by true silence, as if everything in the entire world was holding its breath all at the same time.

Magrit sat up, suddenly scared.

"Hello?" she called, listening to her voice bounce back off the walls, distorted and tiny. "Hello?"

Nobody answered. Not even Master Puppet.

"Oh," she said, her voice echoing inside the vacant spaces. "Oh, no, no, no."

Since her discovery of the skeleton girl, the forbidden quarter of the cemetery had gradually lost its terror for her. Even so, she saw no reason to visit it and had done her best to distract Bugrat away from it. He seemed to love the place, as if it had been carved out of the cemetery for him alone. Magrit did not trust it and they had long since reached a mute understanding. He did not visit it and she did not dwell on the danger she felt still lay within it. But it was his discovery of the skeleton there that had first drawn the world into silence. And now …

"What has he found? What has he found?"

There were no sounds in Magrit's head but the ones she made as she scrambled out of the crypt and ran to the broken gate at the chapel's side. She stopped and called his name.

"Bugrat! Bugrat!"

There was no answer. There was no sound at all. Magrit could feel her breath coming in short, sharp, whimpering bursts. She took one step onto the forbidden ground, then another. When her strength gave way she fell to her hands and knees and crawled, deep into the corner, still calling his name in the hope that she would see a tubby hand waving at her, or the top of his head bobbing above the grass. Only the dry, brown stalks met her gaze, and when she finally managed to drag herself to lie, gasping, next to the skeleton, not even the skeleton girl's voice could be heard.

All Magrit could do was stumble, weeping and terrified, back to the gate and roll onto the welcome grass outside the corner's boundary. But still the sounds of the world would not come. She dried her tears and staggered from one corner of the cemetery to the other, searching for her lost companion. The pile of rags, just behind hers, where they could lie head to head while she whispered silly stories and nonsense rhymes to him as he fell asleep at night, was empty. The broken tomb where he liked to snuggle sometimes, pretending he was dead, lay still and silent. Even the pile of old bones and small rocks he had collected and placed in a corner near the door, which he liked to arrange into patterns and make tiny buildings when it was raining and they had to play inside, sat by itself, with no clue as to his whereabouts. Bugrat wasn't anywhere inside their cold stone home. He had simply disappeared. And still nothing interrupted Magrit's frantic calling.

"Bugrat?" she called again and "Master Puppet?" But not even the voices inside her head were answering and Magrit suddenly missed them very much. She ran outside and looked up at the roof where Master Puppet sat, quiet and unmoving.

"Master Puppet?" she asked, but he did not reply. Instead, he seemed to focus on something off to the side, his eyes wide with horror and his jaw open as if caught in the act of shouting in dismay. Magrit saw the object of his fear, and all the life in her body drained out of her like it had never existed.

Bugrat had dressed and washed himself. He had moistened his hair so it lay flat and neat against his head. He had found a new smock, and brushed the dust and cobwebs from it as best he could. Then he had snuck out of the crypt while Magrit still slept. Now he stood at the edge of the cemetery, on the seat of a plastic tricycle with two broken wheels, which he had placed underneath a window. His face, clean and fresh in the morning light, was pressed up against the glass. One hand was open next to his face. The other was balled up into a fist. Bugrat knocked on the pane: once, twice, three times.

Boom. Boom. Boom.

Like bombs going off in the silence.

Boom. Boom. Boom.

Magrit screamed.

And just like that, the sounds of the world came

crashing back. The frenzied chittering of crickets, the rustle of rats in the grass, the deep, mournful moan of the wind as it caressed the walls of the crypts and the chapel and the surrounding buildings.

And Master Puppet yelling at her,

And the skeleton girl's voice, screaming back, telling him to shut up, that it was time, that this had to happen, to let her go, damn you, let *me* go!

Magrit staggered, overcome by the sheer volume of noise, by its urgency, by the sudden understanding that the universe was panicking, there inside her head, and it was somehow all her fault. Master Puppet was at the front of it, shrieking her name, his voice a mixture of terror and more anger than she had ever heard before; the girl's voice a shrill, staccato counterpoint, her anger and fear rising in opposition to his own.

"You! It's you!" Master Puppet screamed, at the same time the skeleton girl's voice was yelling "Me! It has to be me!" Their voices were mingling together so that, for a moment, it seemed as if the skeleton girl was arguing with herself and Master Puppet had simply chosen a side, choosing to be terrified of discovery instead of demanding it. And in that instant, faced with the same decision, Magrit chose the safety of fear.

"All right," she screeched at them, hands over her ears. "All right!" Bugrat was lifting his fist to knock again. Magrit lurched forwards and wrapped an arm around his chest, lifting him away from the window.

"No!" the skeleton girl screamed, as Master Puppet shrieked a "Yes!" of triumph. Bugrat struggled against Magrit's grip, wriggled to get his limbs free of her embrace. He kicked out, and his foot struck the glass with a dull thud. Magrit froze.

On the other side of the window, four stubby fingers were curling around the edge of the flower-patterned curtain. As Magrit watched, the curtain pulled back. Bugrat stopped kicking and lay limp in her arms, staring at the creature that appeared before them.

A fat, pallid face scowled back at them with piggy eyes. Two teeth poked out from between slug-like lips. It was a boy, perhaps ten or eleven years old. He frowned caterpillar eyebrows straight at them. Behind him, Magrit saw the television flickering. She dimly registered the sound of a favourite tune, one that had lulled her to sleep countless times when she was younger. But there was no comfort in it. There were only the boy's tiny black eyes and Master Puppet's shrill voice screeching at her to "*Get away! Get away!*" And the girl's voice crying "Yes!" like a long, exhausting battle had finally been won. And blood that thudded through her veins and drowned out the noise of their voices.

The boy looked through her to the cemetery beyond, and spent half-a-dozen agonising seconds regarding the crypts and the paths in the dull light. Then his scrutiny passed across the window and discovered Bugrat. His eyes widened. His wet mouth fell open. Magrit heard his voice, thick and slow like a mole poking its head above ground.

"Mum! *Mu-uumm*!"

+✕+

WITH INFINITE AGONY, MAGRIT'S FEET unfroze. She moved one backwards. Then the other. Then a full step, her eyes pinned to the boy in the window. He goggled at Bugrat, ignoring her, that single, terrible word coming from him over and over – "Mum, Mum, Mum," – like drums keeping time to her footsteps. Something moved behind him. Something came out of a door at the far end of the room. Something

huge, covered in a yellow floral dress that simply served to show up how big it was, like a field of daisies that rolled and thudded its way across the floor to stand behind the boy and stare out at Magrit and Bugrat as they fell back, and back, and back.

"OH, MY GOODNESS,"

said Master Puppet, and was silent.

"Oh, thank goodness," said the girl's voice.

The boy's mother dropped a meaty hand upon his shoulder and leaned down, her great potato face gaping out at the cemetery. Four eyes swept across Magrit to focus upon Bugrat. Bugrat slipped from Magrit's grip and stood next to her.

"Oh, my goodness," said the girl's voice, and even though Magrit knew that this was what she wanted, what she had always wanted, her voice held no triumph,

no wicked joy. "Here we go, my beautiful girl."

Magrit ran. She scooped Bugrat up and dashed down the path, away from the awful window and its brightly lit faces. She burst through the door of her favourite crypt, plunged into the nest of rags in the corner, and buried them both as deeply as she could, hiding from the terrible eyes.

"That won't work," said the girl. "They'll find you."

"But where?" Magrit sobbed. "Where?"

"Nowhere," she replied. "This time they're coming!"

Magrit whimpered. She gathered Bugrat up again, ran to the entrance and looked out.

The window was open. Strangers were climbing through.

She heard voices in the cemetery. Strange voices.

Alien voices. The voices of the boy and his mother.

"Look at this!" they were saying, and "Oh, my goodness!" and "Look at *this*!"

Magrit poked her head out the doorway and saw them. They were tramping across her grass, squashing it with their big, flat feet, pushing through neatly piled rubbish bags and knocking them higgledy-piggledy with thoughtless bumps of their elbows and hips.

"Look at this!"

"Oh, my goodness!"

"Look at this!"

They approached the next window down from their own. The mother raised a beefy fist and knocked on it: once, twice, three times. A face appeared; the window opened.

"Look at this!"

"Oh, my goodness!" Another woman, same as the first. She climbed out of the window, turned and called to invisible family members to join her.

Magrit fled. Out the door and on to the next crypt.

"That won't work," said the girl's voice. "They'll find you."

Out again and into the next crypt and the last, in a wide, panicked circle with the girl's voice ringing in her head.

"They'll find you," she cried. "They'll find you."

And on Magrit ran, while the invaders lumbered from window to window, knocking until each pane was opened and more and more giant feet climbed through and thudded down into the grass. They kicked the gravel off the paths. They crushed the flowers. They bent and broke and snapped the rows of vegetable plants she had uncovered, squelched their fruits into the ground and tore their leaves, all the while calling to each other in their thick, meaty voices.

"Look at this!"

"Oh, my goodness!"

"Look at this!"

"Master Puppet!" Magrit cried out, her voice as shrill

and as insubstantial as the wind. "Please, Master Puppet. Help me! Help me, please!"

"I'm sorry." Master Puppet's voice was deep and low and lost in sadness. "This is what you wanted."

"I don't! I don't! I'm sorry. I'm sorry. Please. *Please!*"

There was no going back now, no reclaiming her thoughts and her actions and making it all better. She knew it, and because she knew it, so did Master Puppet.

"You wanted to grow up," he said.

"I didn't. I didn't!"

"Yes, you did. Whether you knew it or not. The moment you accepted Bugrat, the moment you made him your responsibility. The moment you allowed your grown-up thoughts a voice."

"I never did!"

"Didn't you?" And Magrit could hear, in and out and around Master Puppet's voice, the skeleton girl circling.

"You decided to grow up," he said. "This is growing up. I'm so sorry, Magrit. Growing up has consequences."

And then he would answer her no more.

Magrit stared in horror as the hordes invaded her private world. There was nowhere to run. There was nowhere to hide. Everything was uncovered. Everything was ruined. They came on, a wave of flesh that terrified her like nothing she had ever experienced. They leaped from jumpstone to jumpstone. They trundled into the crypts and tore apart her rag nests. They shuffled up and down the gravel paths, their heavy feet scattering small stones. They bumped against her fountains, splashed through her puddles and muddied her washing water without so much as a glance. And Magrit carried Bugrat from corner to corner, barely a step ahead of them: a silent, weeping figure, flitting through the shadows in a desperate attempt to stay hidden.

The intruders found the corner behind the chapel. And they found the dead girl, lying in the grass.

"Oh, my goodness."

"Oh, my goodness."

"Look at that."

"Oh, my goodness."

"They've found me." The girl's voice echoed inside Magrit's head. "I told you they would. They've found me."

"What do I do?" Magrit cried. "What do I do?"

"There's nothing you can do." Master Puppet's voice was quiet. "What will happen must happen."

"But … but …"

She sneaked into the shadows, as the invaders gathered around the shallow grave.

"Who is it?"

"I dunno."

"It's a girl."

"Mebbe."

"Mebbe nowt."

Someone pointed. "It's a girl, it is."

"What do I do?" Magrit whispered.

Two enormous bald men peeled away from the group and squeezed themselves back through a window into an apartment. They returned, shovels in hand. Soon the sound of digging echoed around the cemetery. When they were finished, two more giants appeared, carrying two short planks and a handful of tools. Magrit heard something metal strike something wood. The crowd stood back, and she saw a wooden cross standing above the grass.

"All over now," said a quiet voice inside her head. "All over." The girl's voice, at peace.

"Don't go." Suddenly, Magrit couldn't bear the thought of being without her. "Please, don't go."

But the girl was going and they both knew it.

"Goodbye," she said, fading away. "Thank you."

"Thank you?" Magrit replied. "For what?"

"For giving me a voice," the skeleton replied. "For being me after I was gone. For showing me what I might have become." Then she really *was* gone and not even a gap in the air remained to show that she had ever existed as more than the skeleton of a girl in the grass.

"She was me," Magrit whispered.

"In a way." Master Puppet's voice still held the echo of the skeleton girl, but it was muted now, a part of *him* instead of a part of her that floated about his voice.

"I don't understand."

"Not yet, no."

"If she's me …"

"Why are you still here when she has gone?"

Magrit nodded. Master Puppet sighed, a long, sad sigh that contained too much knowledge.

"You are your own person, Magrit. Echoes outlive the original call."

His voice departed, sliding back out of her head like he was leaving her alone in the dark to sleep, and there was nothing in Magrit's mind except an absence like a deep, deep hole.

And there was a hole in her arms, as well. Magrit blinked. While she was distracted, first by the crowd of strangers and then by the departing voice, Bugrat had wriggled from her grasp. She looked around in sudden panic.

"Bugrat," she hissed. "Bugrat!"

And then she spied him. He was walking across the grass towards his favourite spot, right next to the freshly dug grave. The invaders had their backs turned to him, heads bowed. Magrit gasped.

"Bugrat!"

He was almost upon them. It was only a matter of seconds before they saw him. Magrit looked for some way to recapture him without being seen.

"Bugrat!"

"Magrit." Master Puppet was with her again, his voice soft and gentle, and somehow, oh, so very sad. "Magrit."

"I've got to–" Magrit took a stiff step forwards, then another.

Master Puppet spoke again.

"He'll be seen!"

"Yes." Master Puppet's voice was heavy, like the weight of sadness was crushing it inside his throat. "He will."

"We've got to get him. We've got to get him back."

"Magrit." Something in his tone stopped her, made her lower her arms and stand very still, watching Bugrat wander towards the knot of bodies. "You can't stop him."

"But ... but they'll take him! They'll take him away from me!"

She darted out of the shadows and onto the sunlit lawn. Master Puppet called her name as she dashed across the open space but she ignored him, concentrating only on the little boy ahead of her.

"Bugrat!" She bore down upon him and swooped him up in her arms, then turned to race back to the tiny safety of the dark. Bugrat struggled against her. As she reached the safety of the corner, he kicked out and threw himself away from her grip.

She moved to recapture him but he scooted away

and turned to face her. His face was blood red, his blond hair like a halo around his head. His body stiffened, as if gathering all his energy into one electric ball of defiance, ready to be thrown. He inhaled, and as Magrit's hands moved to cover her mouth, he screamed the only word he would ever say to her.

"No!"

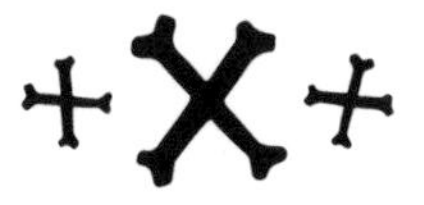

HIS SHOUT RANG OUT, BOUNCED back from the surrounding walls, and echoed over and over in the enclosed space.

The world froze.

The lumbering mob surrounding the grave turned around. Magrit faced them. Magrit saw the ring of faces and placed a protective hand on Bugrat's shoulder. She backed him away: one step, then two. The strangers looked at her. She looked at the strangers.

"Oh. My. Goodness."

"Look at this."

"Oh. My goodness."

The crowd surged towards them. Magrit wanted to run, to race past the corner of the chapel and throw herself into some safe bolthole where she could never be found, where she would never have to suffer the terrible scrutiny of so many tiny piggy eyes all at once. But part of her knew there were no more safe places, that there was nowhere left to hide. She stiffened, and the huge, terrible mass of bodies approached.

"It's a boy!" one of them cried. "A young boy!"

A woman stepped out of the crowd and kneeled down in front of Bugrat.

"Hello," she said softly. "What's your name?"

Magrit grabbed Bugrat's arm, but she couldn't make him move. "Leave him alone!" she yelled, but the strange woman ignored her.

"Don't worry," she said. "I won't hurt you."

"Leave him alone!" Magrit pulled at Bugrat again. Her hands slipped off and she staggered. Just a step. Just a small step. It was enough. The invaders gathered round him, brushing past her as if she was invisible. She retreated, pushed out of the way by their great big legs and their indifference to her presence and their enormous behinds.

"Leave him alone!" she screamed. "He's mine! He's mine!" Nobody heard her. They formed an impenetrable wall between her and Bugrat, cooing and murmuring. Within seconds she could not see him through the forest of meaty legs. She beat at their thick, unyielding backs, but her efforts were like a breeze on the trunks of old oak trees. Nobody so much as waved a hand to ward her off. They simply absorbed her blows as if she did not exist. Finally, she fell back, sobbing.

"Please. Please leave him alone. Please."

The crowd poured towards the gap between chapel and wall, carrying Bugrat along with them, hidden from Magrit's tear-stained face. They slipped into the greater space of the graveyard. Magrit ran after them, but something stopped her at the gap, some force that would let her go no further. She stood, legs trembling, and screamed after them.

"Wait! Wait for me! Please! Please wait for me!"

Nobody waited. Nobody so much as paused. One moment they were before her, a scrum of fleshy bodies and sharp sweat. Then they were gone, out of the cemetery and back through their various windows. And Bugrat was with them and Magrit had not even been able to say goodbye.

She stood in the centre of the patch of grass that had once caused her so much unknowing fear. Now it felt like the only place she belonged, and it was the rest of the graveyard that filled her with dread. Because, for the first time, it seemed horribly large and empty and no longer hers. It belonged to the surrounding buildings and their loud, awful residents. They had invaded it and

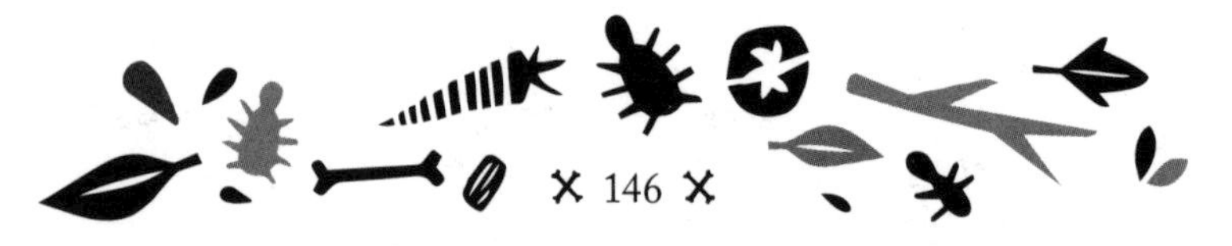

touched it and made it their own and, now, she realised as she turned in a whimpering circle, they had all left their windows open. Their curtains fluttered through the gaps and slapped against the bricks, calling "Ours, ours, ours," in their soft voices. The windows were no longer barriers. They were entrances.

The cemetery was the property of others now. It was part of their world and, in their own unthinking way, they had claimed it. They could, and *would*, climb back through their windows any time they wished. They would wander the grounds at will: naming it, owning it, shaping it to look and sound and feel the way they wanted *their* cemetery to be. She knew – had *always* known – somewhere deep inside her, that it had belonged to others before her arrival, that someone had dug the graves and raised the chapel and laid the paths and called it their own. Then it had, for a short time belonged to Magrit. Now it belonged to someone else again.

And, Magrit understood, there was no place for *her* any more. They had not even seen her, so intent were they on their explorations and the discovery of the boy they stole away from her. They had reclaimed one of their own, and left her behind, rejected.

She retreated from the knowledge, shuffling backwards until her feet caught upon the rough pile of dirt that marked the unknown girl's grave and she slumped down. She leaned her head against the rough wooden cross and wrapped her arms around it as if hugging the neck of the parents she never knew. Her tears found their way down her face and fell to the ground.

"I'm so sorry." The voice that intruded upon her thoughts was soft and gentle. "I tried to warn you. I did not want it to come to this."

"Why?" Magrit opened her eyes, and saw the outline of Master Puppet, high up on his roof, away from the misery that had engulfed her.

"Because, now ..." He paused, and she heard him

sigh, deep inside her. "Now there is no hiding from the truth, and I so wanted you to be able to hide away forever."

"What truth?" She wiped her eyes and gripped the cross even tighter.

"Oh, my poor, poor girl, have you not worked it out?"

Then Master Puppet did something she would never have expected, not in a million years of guessing. He uncurled his arms from the stone cross. He straightened his legs and stood up. As Magrit gaped in shock, he walked along the roof, then climbed down and stood on the grass next to her. He peeled her away from the cross. Then he folded his long cold arms around her and held her against the bones and sticks and twine of his rib cage.

"MY VERY POOR GIRL,"

he said. "I tried to protect you. I really did. But even with all my help and all my advice and all the clever, clever things you learned along the way ..." He turned her so they stared at the grave beneath them, and the girl's body it covered. "When you were four years old, you fell into this cemetery and nobody even noticed, or thought to look for you here when they realised you were gone. You were all alone, with nobody to help you or teach you or kiss you when you were hurt or scared or simply needed to feel arms around you. So you wandered the grounds and learned to survive by touching and tasting and getting pricked and bitten and feeling cold or hot or wet as the seasons demanded. And you found rags to sleep in and shrouds to wear and bones and cans and sticks to build into a friend." Inside her mind, she felt him smile. "And more than a friend: a protector and teacher and parent, when you needed it, and friend when you didn't, yes. And so you learned that weeds tasted horrible and gravel hurt to sleep on and plastic bags tore open and broken books had pictures and all the lessons you needed to survive and grow up and soon you were nine years old, and the world was just a memory." He sighed, like the breath of a dying man, full of loss and regret and the wish that everything had been different.

"When you were almost ten years old, you cut your finger on a rusty tin can, like you had done a hundred times before. And you washed it in the water like you always did and wrapped it in a scrap of rag like you always did and kept it away from dirt and dust like you had learned to do. Only this time, it didn't heal. It grew infected and festered and painful. And slowly, my poor, poor girl, you fell sick and weakened. And one day, quite long ago, you died."

"No."

"You died. You did. I'm so very, very sorry, but there it is. You wandered out to the grass behind the chapel and you lay down and you fell asleep and you never woke up. You died, and your body became a skeleton, and you, you who are a beautiful girl, *my* beautiful girl, you rose up from your dead body, and you have been here with me ever since, nearly ten years old, for fifty and sixty and seventy years and more. Always nearly ten."

"I …" Magrit wanted to argue. But somewhere,

at the bottom of her heart, she knew he was right and that she had always, somehow, known. "If that's my … if that's me …" She reached out and stroked the wooden cross – so real, so hard underneath her fingers – anything rather than think about the bent assembly of bones beneath it. "If that's me … and I've said goodbye and I've gone away …" She looked up at Master Puppet. "How am I still here?"

"Oh, my lovely girl." He ran his stick fingers through her hair.

"But I'm here. With you."

"Yes." He nodded, and held her tighter. "You *are* here. With the friend you built from memories and bones and the voice inside your mind. And we would have stayed here, together, by ourselves. We knew, though, when that baby came. That lively, growing, *living* boy. We knew what had to happen, didn't we?"

Magrit sniffed, and closed her eyes against more tears. "It couldn't last."

"No, my poor girl." Master Puppet stroked her hair. "Not when he was growing older and you never did. Not when he turned two and three and four, and you were always nearly ten. You'll always be nearly ten, no matter how old he becomes. Ghost girls don't age."

"And boys do."

"Real, live, living boys do. And sooner or later they need to be with real, live, living people, who can teach them to talk and live and be alive."

"But … But I touched him and picked him up and held him, and … and …"

"Yes, yes you did. There are some things the living will allow, when they are young and innocent and know no better. But you are still a ghost, my most *lovely* ghost. Ghosts have no sounds to give to the living."

"He could see me. He spoke to me, in the end."

"It is in the nature of living things to see that which isn't real ..." Magrit knew Master Puppet was talking about himself as much as her, and her silent, non-beating heart wept at the thought. "Just as it is in their nature to reject it for the comfort of reality."

"And now he's gone back."

"Yes. Back to real living people and our secret is discovered, and we can't hide any more."

"What will we do?" She looked up at him, at the long, yellow line of his jawbone and the dim pits of his eye sockets as they looked into a distance she could never hope to see. "What can we do?"

He did not move for a long, long time, until Magrit was afraid he would stay that way forever and she would fade away, like the ghost she knew she was, and be forgotten. Then he turned his face down to her and smiled.

"I think it is time," he said, "for us to discover what is beyond these walls, and whether our dreams of rooms and buildings and cemeteries forever are true."

"How?" She frowned in sudden worry.

He nodded to the buildings around them. "The windows are open."

"But ..."

"But what?" He stood and raised her to stand at his side. "You, my dear, are the ghost of a young girl to whom we have already said goodbye.

AND I AM NOTHING MORE THAN THE RESULT OF YOUR IMAGINATION AND WISHES.

And windows that let people in can most *certainly* let ghosts out." He gestured to the surrounding walls. "Pick one!"

Magrit looked around: at the crypts in which she had slept for so many long years; at the paths along which she'd walked; at the overgrown lawns on which she had played. She gazed at the fountains, the jumpstones, the broken, battered, weathered edges of the only world she had ever known. She contemplated the walls that had trapped her, and the sudden choice of exits that flapped curtains at her like a million hands waving goodbye, or hello, or come here! It came to her that the cemetery had fallen silent again – truly silent, the way it had when she had discovered her skeleton lying in the grass, like it had when Bugrat had touched the forbidden windows and forced her world to collide with the larger one outside.

Suddenly, she understood the silence, understood that the dead, the truly dead, have no need for the sounds of the living world, and the world saves its sounds for those who need them. She experienced a flash of overwhelming terror. Then she felt Master Puppet's arm around her shoulder, felt the warmth of his love flowing through her mind, and saw his face looking down at her like it always had: watching over her, *with* her, always with her.

"Listen," he said. Magrit did. Underneath the silence, peeking out like a snail from its shell, she heard the gentle murmur of the world outside the graveyard.

"It's waiting," Master Puppet said.

"ALL YOU HAVE TO DO IS CHOOSE."

"That one," she said, and pointed to a window at random. Master Puppet grinned and squeezed her hand.

"Let's go," he said.

And together, Magrit the ghost girl and her protector, Master Puppet, climbed out of the cemetery and into the world.

ACKNOWLEDGEMENTS

First and foremost, unending thanks and love to my darling wife Lyn and my kids, for the months of nightly "What happens next?" reading sessions, stretched out on my bed, that inspired me to keep going every evening. Thanks also to the staff at Walker Books, especially Sue Whiting, for battering me for just as many months to get the book in some sort of coherent shape, and to my beta readers Paul, Leece and Tehani for their keen eyes and super-valuable critiques. Word up to Catharine Arnold, whose book *Necropolis* provided the pilot light. And grateful thanks to the City of London, for keeping so much of its history alive for me to plunder for my own nefarious ends. And because I swore I would always include a joke to reward anyone who bothered to read the acknowledgements: What do you call a blind dinosaur? A Doyouthinkhesaurus!